"Bellyeoman"
Primary School

Spooky Teachers

D1339928

Tony Bradman

Illustrated by Peter Kavanagh

www.kidsatrandomhouse.co.uk

SPOOKY TEACHERS
A CORGI PUPS BOOK 978 0 552 55347 6

This collection first published in Great Britain by Corgi Pups,
an imprint of Random House Children's Books
This edition published 2005

5 7 9 10 8 6

Collection copyright © Tony Bradman, 2005
Illustrations copyright © Peter Kavanagh, 2005
Cover illustrations © Chris Mould, 2005

The Ghost Teacher
First published in Great Britain by Corgi Pups, 1996
Copyright © Tony Bradman, 1996
Illustrations copyright © Peter Kavanagh, 1996

The Frankenstein Teacher
First published in Great Britain by Corgi Pups, 1998
Copyright © Tony Bradman, 1998
Illustrations copyright © Peter Kavanagh, 1998

The right of Tony Bradman to be identified as
the author of this work has been asserted in accordance
with the Copyright, Designs and Patents Act 1988.

All rights reserved. No part of this publication may be
reproduced, stored in a retrieval system, or transmitted in
any form or by any means, electronic, mechanical, photocopying,
recording or otherwise, without the prior permission of the publishers.

Corgi Pups are published by Random House Children's Books,
61-63 Uxbridge Road, London W5 5SA,
A Random House Group Company

Addresses for companies within The Random House Group Limited
can be found at: www.randomhouse.co.uk/offices.htm

THE RANDOM HOUSE GROUP Limited Reg. No. 954009

A CIP catalogue record for this book is available from the British Library.
Printed and bound in Great Britain by Cox & Wyman Ltd, Reading, Berks

www.**kids**at**randomhouse**.co.uk

The Random House Group Limited makes every effort to ensure that the
papers used in our books are made from trees that have been legally
sourced from well-managed and credibly certified forests. Our paper
procurement policy can be found on www.randomhouse.co.uk/paper.htm.

FSC
Mixed Sources
Product group from well-managed
forests and other controlled sources
www.fsc.org Cert no. TT-COC-2139
© 1996 Forest Stewardship Council

CONTENTS

The Ghost Teacher 1
The Frankenstein Teacher 63

Series Reading Consultant: Prue Goodwin,
Lecturer in Literacy and Children's Books,
University of Reading

THE GHOST TEACHER

Shiver One

This is Sunny Bank Infant and Junior.

It looks like an ordinary school... It certainly *sounds* like an ordinary school... It smells like an ordinary school too, all musty and dusty and chalky, with wandering whiffs of school dinners and disinfectant.

And that's mostly what it is – an ordinary school, a very ordinary school indeed. But wait... something *EXTRA*-ordinary is about to happen here. Something very strange, and very peculiar, and very, very... *SPOOKY*!

Look... there by the dustbins, what do you see? A shimmering and a glimmering, and a figure forming in the darkness.

It is The Ghost Teacher, and
her name is Miss Shade.

She glides over to a window, and peers in...

"Class Three! *Class Three*!" Somebody was trying hard to make herself heard above an absolutely terrible din. "Will you *please* be quiet and behave! I'm warning you, this is *definitely* your last chance..."

"Oh dear, things are much, much worse than I thought," whispered Miss Shade. "I only hope I'm not too late..."

Then she slid... *through* the wall and into the school. She drifted down a corridor...

wafted round a corner... then slipped through a keyhole. She was in the classroom where the absolutely terrible din was coming from.

No-one there could see her... not yet, anyway. But she could see them. And Class Three were doing what they did best – behaving badly.

They got up to the usual things, of course – dreaming when they should be working,

fidgeting when they should be sitting still,

chattering when they should be listening,

picking their noses and flicking it at each other.

They did much more, though.

They did lots
of pulling and
prodding
and poking.

They did lots
of crashing and
bashing and
practical joking.

They did lots
of fighting
and biting
and writing...

but only
on the wall.

This is what Class Three's classroom looked like at nine o'clock on the first morning of term.

This is what it looked like just *one hour* later.

And this is... what Class Three look like. They're shocking, aren't they?

Class Three made more noise than the rest of Sunny Bank Infant and Junior School put together. They were more trouble than a barrel full of babies. In short, Class Three were... a teacher's worst nightmare.

This is Miss Nicely, Class Three's teacher. She was trying to do what *she* did best – teaching Class Three all sorts of interesting stuff.

But Class Three, as usual, weren't taking any notice of her. And Miss Nicely was feeling fed up. She was fed up with shouting. She was fed up with not being listened to. She was very fed up with Class Three.

This is what Miss Nicely looked like at nine o'clock on the first morning of term.

This is what she looked like just *one hour* later.

And this is an extreme close-up of what she looks like today. It's shocking, isn't it?

Suddenly, something snapped inside her.

She grabbed her handbag and headed towards the door. For once, Class Three *did* take notice.

"Hey, Miss!" they called out, rudely. "Where are you going?"

Then she slammed the door shut behind her, and strode off down the corridor. Miss Shade slid through the classroom wall, and wafted along after Miss Nicely. They could both hear Class Three... cheering.

This is Mr Dickens, headteacher of Sunny Bank Infant and Junior.

He looks like an ordinary headteacher. He sounds like an ordinary headteacher. He smells like an ordinary headteacher too, all musty and dusty and chalky, with wandering whiffs of school dinners and disinfectant.

And that's exactly what he is, an ordinary headteacher, a very ordinary headteacher indeed. At that precise moment he was *head*ing down the corridor too, and he was about to bump into Miss Nicely.

"Not any more, there isn't," said Miss Nicely. "I resign, Mr Dickens. You can find somebody else to be Class Three's teacher from now on."

And with that, she swept out of the school.

A horrified Mr Dickens watched her go. He listened to Class Three creating havoc in the distance, and a frown crossed his face. Then he turned and marched off to his office, looking very, *very*... determined.

"Umm," murmured Miss Shade. "Time I got to work..."

Miss Shade glided along the corridor to Class Three's classroom, where the din was even more terrible than before. She waited outside for a moment, listening and tutting. Then she slid in through the... *closed* door.

And this time she made sure everyone there could see her.

Class Three were rather surprised by her... *appearance*. In fact, they were so surprised, they stopped having a riot. They went very quiet indeed.

This is what they looked like before Miss Shade appeared.

And this is what they looked like *one second* later. They froze in the middle of whatever naughtiness they were up to.

They look shocked, don't they?

"Good morning, Class Three,"

said Miss Shade. Class Three didn't reply, although some of them did close their mouths. "My name is Miss Shade, and I will be standing in for Miss Nicely. We've got lots to do, so..."

said somebody brave.

"Of course I am!" said Miss Shade. There was a sharp intake of breath from the entire class. "Now, settle down, everybody," continued Miss Shade. "I'm going to..."

The entire class trembled...

Class Three stopped trembling, and breathed out in relief.

said the brave child.

She clicked her ghostly fingers, and it went dark. Strange, haunting noises filled the air. Peculiar wisps of light appeared from everywhere.

And Miss Shade gave off a...*spooky* glow.

everybody in Class Three wailed. They hugged each other in fright, but Miss Shade took absolutely no notice of them.

"Once upon a time," she said, in a voice that made the little hairs stand up on the backs of the children's necks, "there was a school, a very ordinary school.

But in that school there was a badly behaved class..."

As Class Three watched, the wall behind Miss Shade turned blurry, began to fade, then vanished completely. A phantom classroom appeared, and with a gasp, Class Three recognized the people in it straightaway.

"Hey, *that's us*!" they yelled, amazed.

"In fact, they were absolutely *awful*," continued Miss Shade. "They never allowed their poor, poor teacher a moment's peace. They misbehaved the whole time. And I'm sorry to say they did some *terrible* things..."

The phantom classroom before Class Three wobbled, and changed. Soon Class Three were watching something like a film on fast forward. And they saw everything they had got up to since the first day of term.

They saw all the pulling and prodding and poking. They saw all the crashing and bashing and practical joking. They saw all the fighting and biting. And they definitely saw all the writing on the wall.

None of them said a word. But as they sat there in the darkness watching themselves, some of Class Three *did* feel slightly... ashamed.

The phantom film slowed, then cut to a vision of Miss Nicely working at home.

"But the class didn't give a hoot."

Now some more of Class Three felt quite... ashamed.

"Then one day," said Miss Shade, "the class behaved *so* badly, their poor, poor teacher couldn't stand it a minute longer. She left, and started looking for another job, any job... provided it didn't involve children."

At last, the whole of Class Three felt very ashamed indeed. Although that didn't stop one or two of them from still being rather... cheeky.

"Here, Miss!" a voice called out. "This story isn't very scary!"

"Don't worry," said Miss Shade. "We're just getting to the scary part... The head of the school had to find someone to replace the poor, poor teacher.

So he decided to put an advertisement in the newspaper."

The vision of Miss Nicely wobbled, and changed into a picture of Mr Dickens writing at his desk:

Then the phantom picture went into fast forward again.

Class Three watched as the newspaper was printed, teachers read the advertisement and replied, then came to be interviewed for the job by Mr Dickens. "Finally, the head found the person he was looking for," said Miss Shade. "Someone who would keep you under control, someone who wouldn't stand for any nonsense. In short, Class Three – your worst nightmare..." Class Three gulped at the vision before them.

It was a teacher with a beaky nose and an even beakier chin. It was a teacher with a tight little bun and an even tighter little mouth. It was a teacher with steely blue eyes that saw... *everything*.

And her name was... *Miss Stern*. A phone rang in the phantom film. Miss Stern reached out and answered it. Her voice made Class Three instantly sit up straight.

Hello, Mr Dickens. I've got the job? Thank you, that's wonderful news. Yes, I'll be there tomorrow. I can hardly wait to get started on Class Three — especially the cheeky ones you mentioned...
WINNER

Miss Stern put the phone down, and slowly turned to stare at Class Three. The phantom film froze with her eyes drilling into them. A few of the children - probably the cheeky ones - let slip little moans.

"I only wish I could," said Miss Shade, sadly. "But alas, I can't. You have seen your past, Class Three, and what is happening in the present. You have also seen your future, and that cannot be changed. Unless..."

"Unless what, Miss?" several voices called out, eagerly.

"Unless," said Miss Shade, "you change... *yourselves*. You *could* give up the pulling and prodding and poking, the crashing and bashing and practical joking, and the fighting and biting and writing on the wall..."

"We can't!" said a voice. "We *love* doing that stuff! It's what we do best, isn't it, everybody?"

There was much murmuring of agreement.

"Oh well," said Miss Shade with a sigh.

"If that's the way you feel, I won't argue. But you'd better get used to how things are going to be..." Miss Shade clicked her ghostly fingers.

Suddenly, Miss Stern's phantom film face came to life once more.

"Right, Class Three!" she snapped. "Silence! No play-time until you've finished all the difficult sums..."

"OK, we surrender!" yelled Class Three, remembering too the shame they'd felt at seeing what they'd done. "Please, help us to get Miss Nicely back," one of them added. "We'll do *anything* you say."

"Cross your hearts and hope to die?" asked Miss Shade.

"If we don't, we'll eat worm pie!" chanted Class Three.

"I'm glad to hear it," said Miss Shade, clicking her ghostly fingers again. The darkness was replaced by light, and the wall returned to normal. "Right, you can make a start by tidying this classroom. It's a *disgrace*..." Class Three set to work with a will.

This is what the classroom looked like when they began.

This is what it looked like just *one hour* later.

And this is Class Three looking a bit shocked at being so well behaved.

"What do you think, Miss?" said somebody, proudly.

"I think you never know what you can do until you've tried, Class Three," replied Miss Shade. "Wouldn't you agree? Now I want you all to sit down, fold your arms, and prepare to say something very important."

Miss Shade clicked her fingers one last time. Soft, sprinkly, tinkling sounds came from everywhere, and then... a dazed Miss Nicely appeared out of thin air. Miss Shade made sure Miss Nicely couldn't see her.

"Oh, no," Miss Nicely groaned, and closed her eyes. "I can't stand it!"

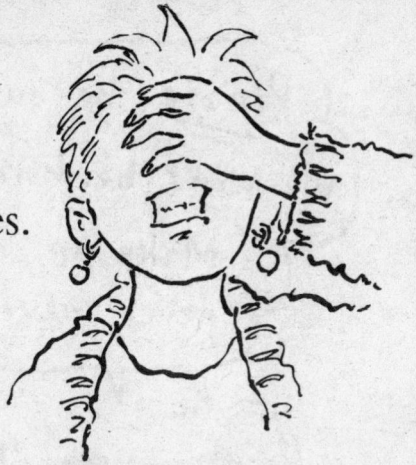

"Come on, Class Three," whispered Miss Shade. "Say the magic words..."

"*Sorry*, Miss Nicely!" said someone. Other voices joined in, and soon the whole of Class Three was apologizing.

Miss Nicely opened her eyes. She looked as if she'd just woken from her worst nightmare. She smiled, faintly.

Then Mr Dickens came in.

"Ah, you're back, Miss Nicely," he said, and dropped a crumpled piece of paper in the bin. "I see you've got everything under control here, too. Nicely done, Miss Nicely. Keep up the good work, Class Three!"

"I couldn't have put it better myself," whispered Miss Shade. She smiled, waved goodbye... and slipped out through the keyhole.

"Who said that?" asked Mr Dickens.

But nobody told him...

That's more or less the end of this story. Class Three *did* keep up the good work, except for some dreaming and fidgeting and chattering and nose picking and flicking. Miss Nicely didn't mind all that, though.

She wasn't *quite* sure what had happened. But compared to how they'd been before, Class Three were... *angels*, so she wasn't complaining.

And what, you ask, became of Miss Shade? Well, as long as there's a class misbehaving somewhere, there's no rest for The Ghost Teacher.

Which means the next school
to get a SPOOKY visit is...
BOUND TO BE YOURS!

THE FRANKENSTEIN TEACHER

Chapter One

High in the spooky mountains, a spooky storm was raging. In the heart of that spooky storm, there stood a spooky old castle. In that spooky old castle, there was a spooky laboratory. And in that spooky laboratory . . .

Something very, very *spooky* was going on.

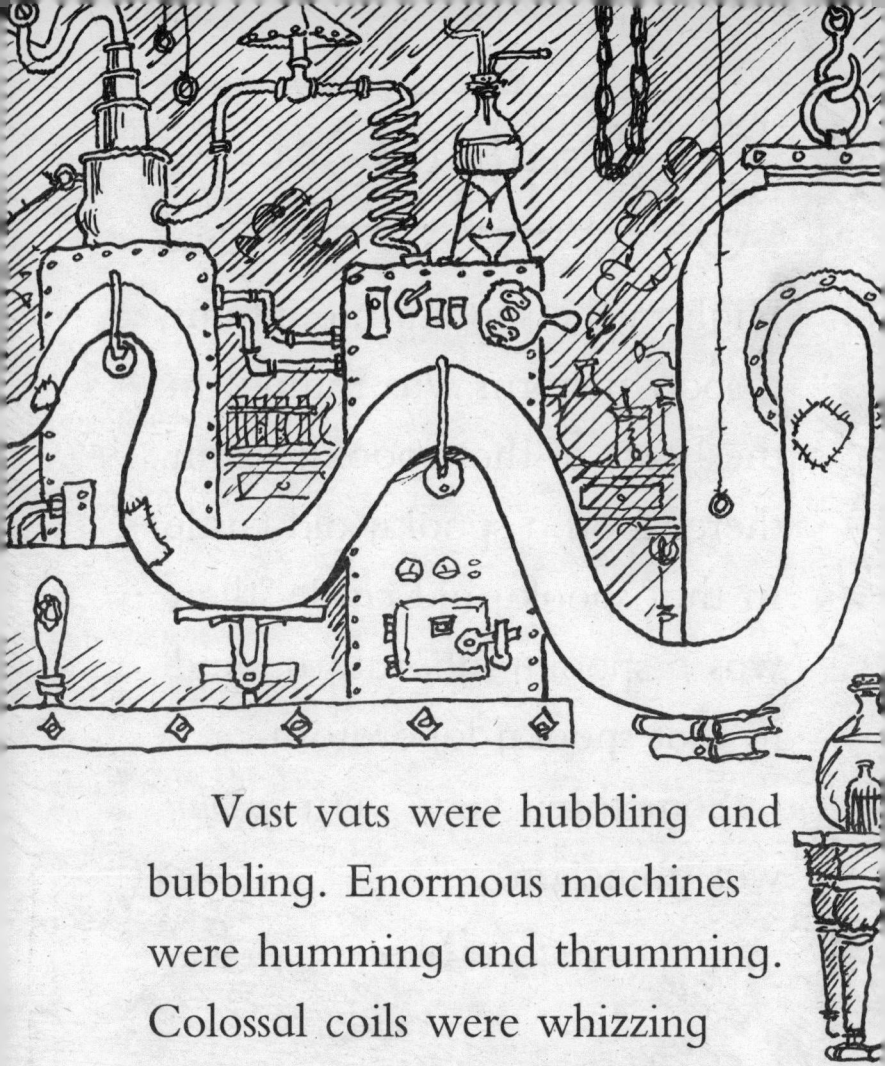

Vast vats were hubbling and bubbling. Enormous machines were humming and thrumming. Colossal coils were whizzing and fizzing. And right in the middle of all that sound and fury was . . . The Doctor.

He pulled a massive lever.

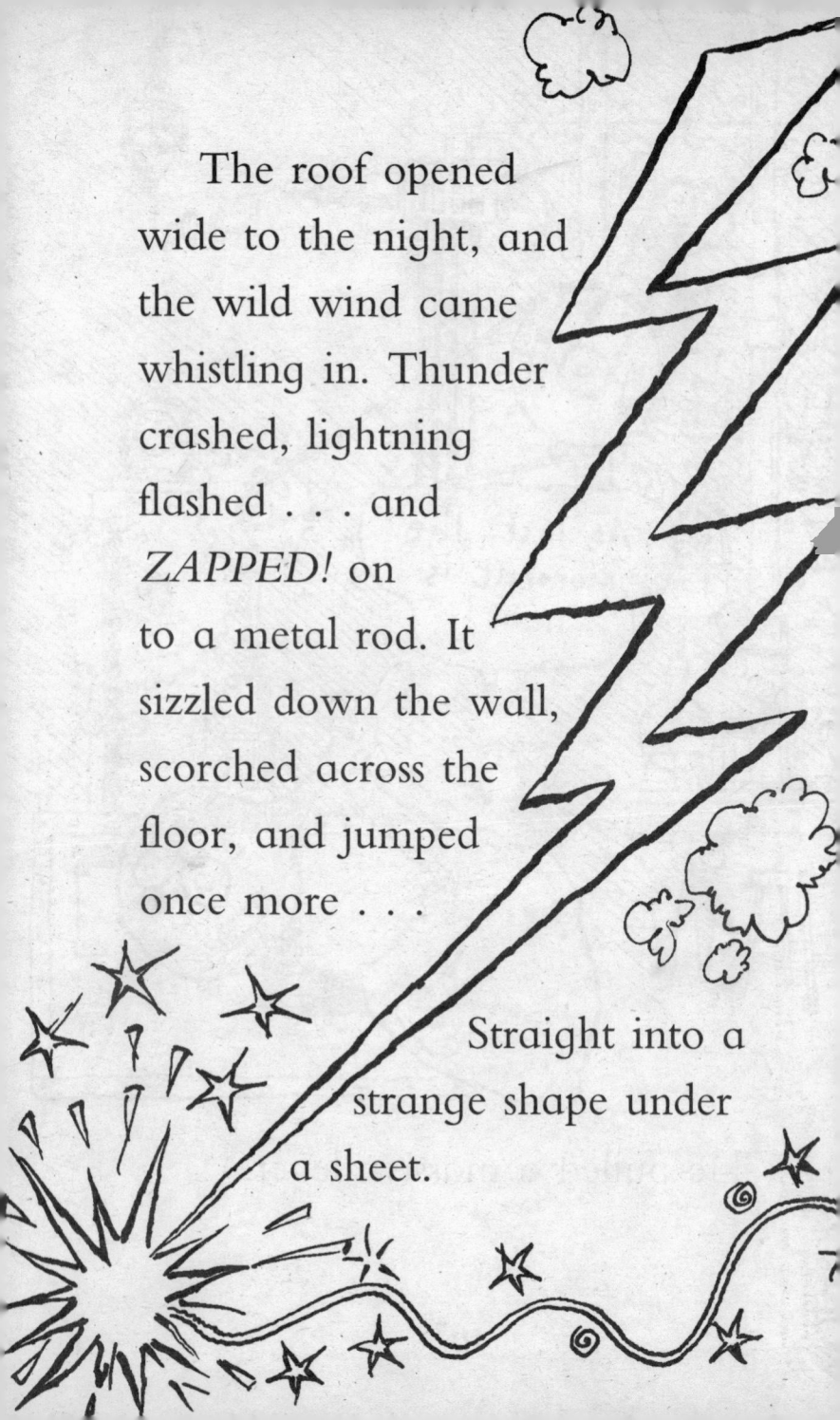

The roof opened wide to the night, and the wild wind came whistling in. Thunder crashed, lightning flashed . . . and *ZAPPED!* on to a metal rod. It sizzled down the wall, scorched across the floor, and jumped once more . . .

Straight into a strange shape under a sheet.

The Doctor threw some switches. Bright sparks flew, choking smoke billowed, and The Doctor checked his dials. He looked around – and then he smiled. Beneath the sheet there were definitely some . . . twitches.

MY CREATION LIVES!

Suddenly, the shape sat up and the sheet fell away. A hideous creature was revealed. The creature rose to its giant feet. It stamped stiffly towards The Doctor.

It reached out with its giant hands. It moaned and it groaned.

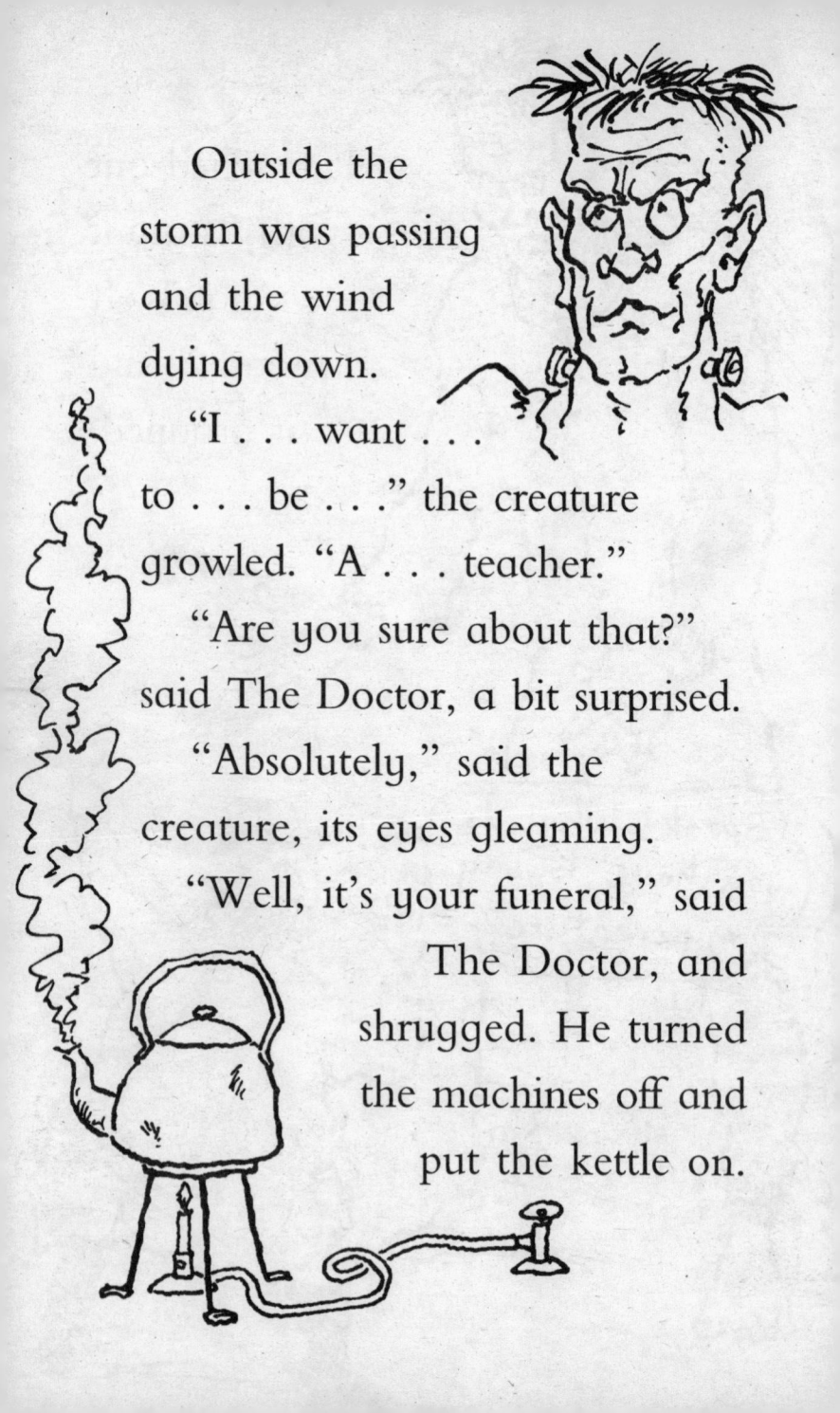

Outside the storm was passing and the wind dying down.

"I . . . want . . . to . . . be . . ." the creature growled. "A . . . teacher."

"Are you sure about that?" said The Doctor, a bit surprised.

"Absolutely," said the creature, its eyes gleaming.

"Well, it's your funeral," said The Doctor, and shrugged. He turned the machines off and put the kettle on.

Personally, I can't stand kids, and I can't think of a worse job. But somebody's got to do it, I suppose.

So The Doctor got the creature into Teacher Training College. The creature worked hard, and one day he wasn't just a creature any more. He had a posh piece of paper that said he was . . .

Now all he needed was a class to teach . . .

Chapter Two

Down at the foot of the spooky mountains, there was a little town. At the edge of that little town, there stood a little school. At the heart of that little school, there was a little classroom. And in that little classroom . . .

Something very, very *little* had escaped.

Most of the children were laughing and cheering. A few of them were screaming and squealing. Two of them were chasing and leaping.

And right in the middle of all that sound and fury was . . . Mrs Shelley, the head.

Hannibal the class hamster had made a break for freedom.

But now he was almost trapped. He ducked and dived, he weaved and bobbed, he scampered this way and that across the floor, then jumped once more . . .

Straight into the cage from where he'd started.

"Thank goodness for that," said Mrs Shelley, shutting the cage door with a *PING!* "I'd better speak to your new teacher about Hannibal," she said. "I don't want him causing as much chaos in the school as he did last term."

"Who is our new teacher, Miss?" asked one of the children.

"You'll soon find out," said Mrs Shelley. "Ah, I think I hear him now."

The children listened. There was a *THUD!* outside in the corridor. Then another, and another . . .

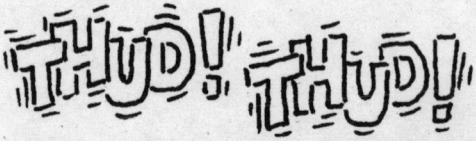

Somebody was heading steadily towards their classroom. Somebody with *very* heavy feet, it seemed.

The floor shook. The tables and chairs shook. The *children* shook.

Suddenly, the door creaked open . . . and a huge figure loomed over them. It was . . .

...the FRANKENSTEIN teacher!

The class gasped, and shook even more. Hannibal squeaked, and fell off his exercise wheel.

"Pay attention please, everybody," said Mrs Shelley. "This is your new teacher, Mr Frankenstein, which makes you class 3F, of course. Now, what do we say, Class 3F? We say, *Good morning, Mr Frankenstein.*"

Mrs Shelley waited. But Class 3F just sat there, shaking and silent.

"Come along, children," said Mrs Shelley. "Where are your manners?"

Class 3F didn't say a word. They were totally stunned.

"That's not a very nice welcome, Class 3F," said Mrs Shelley crossly. "I hope you're just shy today. Well, I'll leave them in your capable hands, Mr Frankenstein," she said, turning to leave. "I'm sure everything will be fine."

Mrs Shelley couldn't have been more wrong if she'd tried.

Chapter Three

At the front of the little classroom, there stood The Frankenstein Teacher in his big suit. Inside that big suit, there was his big body. Inside that big body, there beat his big heart.

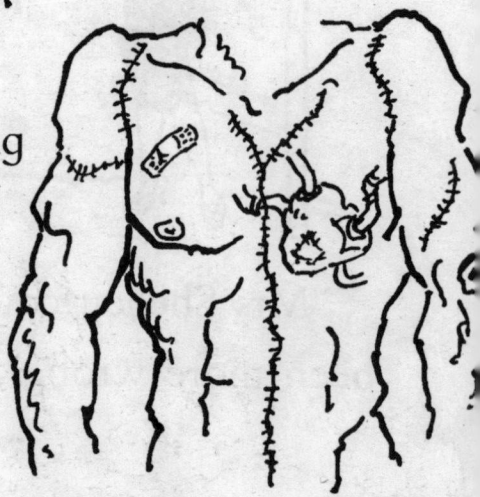

And inside that big heart . . .

Something very, very . . . *big* was being felt.

After all, this was the biggest day of The Frankenstein Teacher's life. Unlike The Doctor, The Frankenstein Teacher *loved* kids. He couldn't think of a better job than being a teacher. He was desperate to do it well.

He was desperate for the kids to like him, too.

The children of Class 3F were starting to relax, at least. Most of them were staring at The Frankenstein Teacher. But a few of them were whispering to each other. And two of them actually put their hands up.

"Er . . . yes?" said The Frankenstein Teacher, in

his growly voice. He pointed at the nearest child who wanted to ask a question.

"Why are you so . . . ugly, Sir?" said the child, a cheeky boy. The class exploded into sniggers and giggles, and relaxed a whole lot more.

"Excuse me?" said The Frankenstein Teacher, a bit surprised.

"Please, Sir!" called out the second child with a hand up.

"Yes?" said The Frankenstein Teacher, turning to her.

"Hannibal's escaped again, Sir!" she said, and the same old panic began.

Pretty soon most of the children were laughing and cheering, a few of them were screaming and squealing, and two of them were chasing and leaping. And right in the middle of all that sound and fury was . . .

The not-so-happy Frankenstein Teacher, doing his best.

He helped catch Hannibal. He stamped stiffly round the classroom with his giant feet,

THUD! THUD! THUD!

He reached out with his giant hands. He held on to the hamster . . . and gently eased him back in his cage.

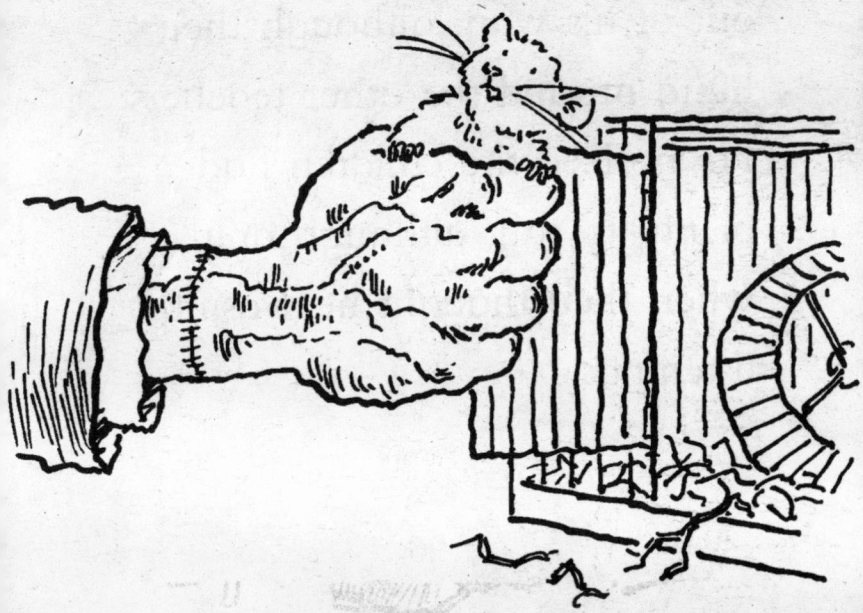

But that word *ugly* kept ringing through his brain.

He noticed the children kept out of his way, although they hung around the other teachers. He noticed the children had plenty to say, although only when they thought he wasn't listening.

And by the end of the day . . .

The Frankenstein Teacher
was *very* . . . depressed.

"They don't like me, Hannibal," he said sadly to the only friend he'd made. "It's because of how I look, isn't it?" Hannibal peeked in his mirror too, and squeaked.

"Though I suppose I could change that, couldn't I . . . ?"

On the opposite edge of the little town from the school, there stood a shiny new shopping mall. In the heart of that shiny new shopping mall, there was a shiny new clothes shop. And in that shiny new clothes shop . . .

Something very, very . . . *shiny and new* was being tried on.

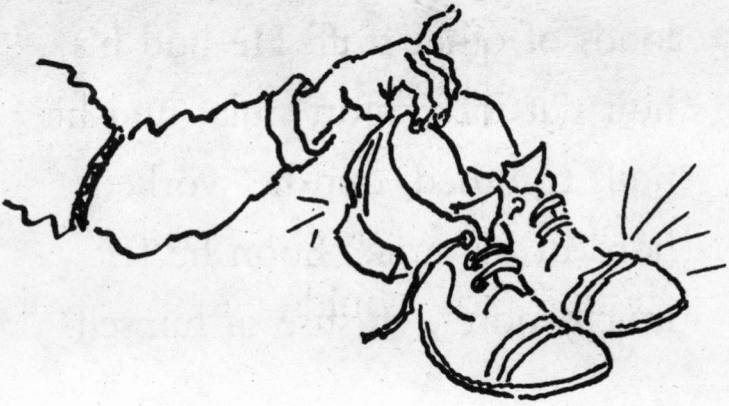

So The Frankenstein Teacher bought the shiny new suit, and loads of other stuff. He had his hair cut in a smart style, and his nails trimmed, and he worked hard at his smile. Soon he felt much more . . . sure of himself.

Now all he needed was a certain class's approval . . .

The next morning, the classroom filled up as usual. Class 3F sat and waited for their teacher . . . and waited . . . and waited.

The children listened.

Somebody was heading steadily towards the classroom. Someone who still had very heavy feet.

The floor shook. The tables and chairs shook. The *children* shook.

Suddenly the door creaked open . . . and a huge figure stood framed in the light. It was The Frankenstein Teacher, grinning for all he was worth.

The class gasped, and shook even more . . . only with *laughter* this time.

Hannibal squeaked and fell off his exercise wheel again. But nobody noticed. Class 3F was too busy laughing at the person in front of them.

"Er . . . OK, Class 3F," he growled at last, still smiling. "What's the joke?"

"You are, Sir," a boy spluttered, and the class howled, until the whole school could hear them. The Frankenstein Teacher didn't say a word.

But the smile slowly faded from his face.

Chapter Five

Across the gloomy sky, some gloomy clouds were gathering. Beneath those gloomy clouds, there stood a gloomy school. In that gloomy school, there was a gloomy head's office. And in that gloomy head's office . . .

Something very, very . . . *gloomy* was happening.

After all, this was the gloomiest moment of The Frankenstein Teacher's life. He'd tried hard to do a good job. He'd done his best to make the children like him. But their laughter kept ringing through his brain.

So he had decided to give up being a teacher.

"Are you sure about that?" said Mrs Shelley, a bit surprised. The Frankenstein Teacher nodded gloomily. "Oh, well," said Mrs Shelley, rather sadly. "I hope you'll stay with us for the rest of the day, at least."

The Frankenstein Teacher trudged back to the classroom with Mrs Shelley,

THUD! THUD! THUD!

Mrs Shelley told Class 3F the news.

But Class 3F weren't impressed. In fact, they couldn't see what the fuss was about. How could somebody so *ugly* be worth having? They just wanted a new teacher. Any teacher who was better looking.

And who wore nice, sensible teacher clothes.

The clock ticked on, and time slid past, until home time came around at last. Then, with a sigh, The Frankenstein Teacher said goodbye . . . and left.

At the school gates, grown-ups were moaning and groaning. Children were teasing and squeezing. Babies were squalling and bawling. And right in the middle of all that sound and fury was . . . a hamster on the run.

"Quick, after him!" shouted a boy, and Class 3F gave chase.

But Hannibal kept up a furious pace. He ducked and dived, he weaved and bobbed, he searched this way and that for a pair of heavy feet. And there they were, heading steadily along . . . the other side of the street!

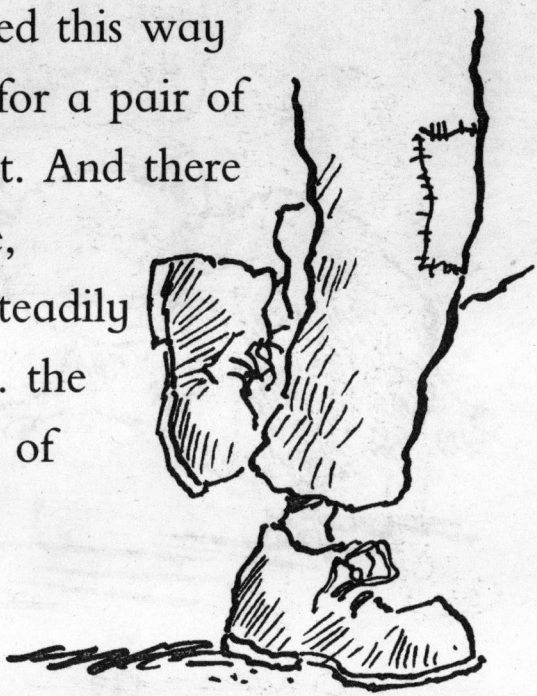

Hannibal paused. The children were closing in on him from behind, and thoughts of road safety fled from his mind. Hannibal rushed out to follow his friend, and then with a . . . *SPLAT!* – he met a swift end.

Mrs Shelley had run him over with her car.

Chapter Six

It was an accident, of course, and poor Mrs Shelley was very upset. The children were stunned and pale. A few of them had started to wail.

Two of them were saying that somebody should take Hannibal to the vet.

"I think it's too late for that," growled The Frankenstein Teacher.

He stamped swiftly through the crowd of people with his giant feet . . .

He reached out with his giant hands. He picked up the little splattered hamster. He held Hannibal gently in his giant arms.

A giant tear rolled down his cheek.

And that's when Class 3F saw that there was more to their ex-teacher than met the eye. He might be ugly, but he felt sad enough to cry! So under that hideous surface, he must be a . . . *pretty nice guy.*

Just then, thunder boomed, and lightning split the sky.

"No," said The Frankenstein Teacher. "But I know a man who can."

High in the spooky mountains, a spooky storm was raging. In the heart of that spooky storm, there stood a spooky old castle. In that spooky old castle, there was a spooky laboratory. And in that spooky laboratory . . .

You know *exactly* what kind of spookiness was going on.

There was hubbling and bubbling and humming and thrumming and whizzing and fizzing and crashing and flashing and *ZAPPING* and sizzling and switching and some twitching . . . in a strange little shape under a sheet.

"It lives!" The Doctor shouted. And The Frankenstein Teacher smiled.

He did a lot more smiling later. Back at school, Class 3F were waiting for him. This time he got a much nicer welcome, especially when the children saw that Hannibal was . . . OK! Mrs Shelley was very relieved.

Hannibal looked a bit different from the way he used to before he was splattered. Though now Class 3F realized . . . *how you look doesn't matter.*

"Three cheers for Mr Frankenstein, the best teacher in the world!" somebody yelled.

The Frankenstein Teacher didn't know what to say.

But he knew in his big heart, this was truly . . . his happiest day!